Ms. Grace
Gives a Party

Written by
Charles Flynn Hirsch

Illustrated by
Deborah Colvin Borgo

Highlights for Children , Inc.

"Tomorrow I'm going to have a party!"
Ms. Grace told her friends.

"Oh, good," said Sir Good.

"But why?" asked Baby Di.

"Why? Why, because it's spring," answered
Ms. Grace.

Which picture shows Ms. Grace's spring garden?

What do the other pictures show?

"We've got much to do," continued Ms. Grace. "Why? Because we're going to have a party!"

"Why? Why, because it's spring!" sang Baby Di and Sir Good.

"Here's how we'll make the invitations," said Ms. Grace.

"Very good," said Sir Good.

"Take colored paper. Cut it out in the shape of an egg."

"And then, cut out a long stem from green paper."

"Next, cut out 2 big green leaves, just like the shape of my ears."

"Paste the egg shape to the top of the stem. Paste the 2 leaves to the bottom."

"Let's write when and where the party will be on these invitations. Then we can send them to our friends," said Ms. Grace.

"Please deliver these invitations to Jack Koala and Ketchup O'Leary," said Ms. Grace. "I hope they'll join us."

Which way should Sir Good go to find Jack?
Which way should Baby Di go to find Ketchup O'Leary?
Trace each path with your finger.

What happened first? Next? Last?

What would you do to help Ms. Grace?

"Oh my, oh me. My best dishes are in pieces," said Ms. Grace.

But Ms. Grace's cheery song went sad.

"Tra-la, tra-la, to do my party dishes,"
Ms. Grace sang happily.

At that moment Baby Di and Sir Good returned.
"Here, fair lady," said Sir Good. "Use my superduper,
sticky glue to mend your dishes. It's very good for putting
together broken castles and kings' crowns."

**Help Ms. Grace and her friends glue the dishes back together.
What pieces go together?**

"Oh, dribble drabble,"
Ms. Grace muttered.
"One of my cups is in
pieces. I'll go without."

**How many friends will be
at the party?
How many cups are there?
Who will go without?**

"Now off with you. Sleep well tonight," said Ms. Grace. "Tomorrow we're going to have a party."

"Oh me, oh my. Tomorrow is today. Now I must make wonderful party things to eat," said a very excited Ms. Grace.

"Scoop the flour from the bin."

FLOUR

"Roll the dough until it's thin."

"Place the crust on the plate."

"Slide the pie in to bake."

"Rhubarb pie will add to the fun.
I can't wait until it's done."

Show how you would make a pie as Ms. Grace does.

"Such wonderful things to eat," said Ms. Grace. And she began to taste the goodies that she had made.

Where did the food on Ms. Grace's tray come from?

"Oh me, oh my," cried Ms. Grace. "But what a mess I've made!"

What should Ms. Grace do first?
What should she do next?
What should she do after that?
And what should Ms. Grace do last?

Ms. Grace looked at all the wonderful things around her house. She asked, "What can I use to make the house pretty?"

What might Ms. Grace use?

"Dear, dear," sighed Ms. Grace. "I seem to have misplaced a few things."

Help Ms. Grace find her

glasses

bows

candles

spoons

flowers

Ms. Grace waited for her friends, who came from near and far. Ketchup O'Leary swung in from her place. And Jack flew in from Chicago.

Which friends came *over* something to come to Ms. Grace's house?
Which friends came *under* something?

"Hi," said Jack.
"Hello, my sweet," said Ketchup O'Leary.
"Let's sing, 'Happy spring,' " sang Baby Di.
"Good day, my lady," said Sir Good Knight.

"Oh my, a present for me?" asked Ms. Grace.
"But why? It's not my birthday."

"Why? Because you broke a favorite cup," said Baby Di.

"Why? Because we love you, Ms. Grace," all her friends joined in.